# SEA
## OF
# RED

ALEXANDRA MATHER

authorHOUSE®

*AuthorHouse™ UK*
*1663 Liberty Drive*
*Bloomington, IN 47403 USA*
*www.authorhouse.co.uk*
*Phone: 0800 047 8203 (Domestic TFN)*
*+44 1908 723714 (International)*

*Published by AuthorHouse  12/02/2019*

*ISBN: 978-1-7283-9650-7 (sc)*
*ISBN: 978-1-7283-9649-1 (e)*

CHAPTER

It was a lovely sunny day, birds were singing as I reached my car. For the first time for a long time I felt happy and relaxed I had struggled through the last few years since my husband had left but had managed to buy myself a nice little flat that I had furnished, I decided that I was going to sell everything that reminded me of my past life and had certainly made a start on that, selling a lot of things online and the rest to the charity shop. I wanted to be free of any clutter. All my Steiff bears had gone which was sad but necessary. Anything else, once the summer came would be taken to a car boot sale, which I always feel is a very good way to get rid of things that you don't need-maybe someone else can find a home for them.

The flat was very tidy that morning, for a change, I had cleaned the floor, bathroom, kitchen were all in pristine condition, all clean and tidy. Even the windows were cleaned the week before. It was like a new beginning.

I eased my tatty little car into gear and set off down the road. I had to pop into the local Waitrose to pick up my newspaper and my coffee of course which was given away free! Did that without spilling it everywhere which was a first for me as it was constantly tipping out, burning my fingers etc.

However, I turned out of Waitrose and set off towards Old Basing, a lovely place in Hampshire, very old going back to Cromwellian times seeped in history

I travelled on to reach the A30. When I drove onto it the road was clear, music playing quite loudly, lovely day sun shining. As I travelled along the road opens up and the grass verge in the centre disappears. I reached the hotel on the left and slowed down slightly remembering the day I had gone there to drop off leaflets for the unit that I used to visit.

Then- out of nowhere comes an enormous lorry, swerving all over the road. He must have have lost control seemed like he was speeding. Then, the crash, then silence, complete silence. My little car was no more- completely crushed under the lorry. I didn't know where I was, I was looking down on the lorry, and the driver must have hit his head on the steering wheel, as he was completely motionless. I could see a lot of red colour must be blood pouring from my body under the lorry. Good lord, 8 pints we have in our bodies- it was like a sea of red! Pumping out is the only way I could describe it like when you go to fill your car at the petrol station it seemed to be spilling out everywhere. Seems never ending.

Suddenly there is a noise –sirens -Police? Ambulance? Fire Brigade? Again the red colour of the Fire Brigade. Men running all over the place. I heard a voice say "They can't possibly have lived through this" But I was fine floating about seeing what was going on. I so did try to tell them but I don't think they were listening. My son used to say I could be very nosy at times, the need to know things, but on this occasion I felt it was necessary.

At the time I was worried about the state of the lorry driver who hadn't moved at all. All I could see was his hair, which was blonde and so thick, but his head was still down on the steering wheel, I did wonder whether he was breathing. Surely they could give him the kiss of life but at that point they seemed more interested in my car, or what was left of it.

I found I could move in a little closer as I was getting quite worried about the lorry driver who was still sitting motionless in his seat. As I got closer I noticed his tattoos and jewellery, quite a lot of it. I moved closer still trying to see if he was breathing. As I did so he suddenly opened his eyes, blue grey I think they were. It was a relief to see his eyes open even though he didn't seem to see me and didn't hear me when I spoke to him. He was very nice looking and even though I couldn't see his body he looked quite tall.

They seemed to spend so long with my car, I am not there I kept screaming at them, look at the driver!

At last they decided to come and see him and check on him, the policeman stood there assessing whether he could speak or not "What the hell happened?" He said in quite a deep midlands voice, I gathered from this he came from somewhere near to Birmingham. The policeman helped him out of the lorry and I was right he was tall! He looked so upset I wanted to put my arms around him and tell him I was all right and not to worry. The poor man-I felt so sorry for him. He kept saying he didn't know what had happened, one minute he was driving along and the next minute he was over the other side of the road, he could see me travelling towards him and there was nothing he could do. The lorry wouldn't stop however hard he tried. He was muttering that he had been driving lorries for years and had never had an accident until today.

He was taken away by the police, I don't think he had been arrested or anything it was an accident and I think they believed him.

An enormous truck arrived I presume to hoist the lorry up. They then began the horrible task of getting the lorry off my car. The blood still seemed to be running everywhere; shattered glass was strewn all over the place. The air bags they were using were enormous they lifted the lorry upwards and they were able to assess my car and I guess me! My body was black probably from the oil in the car mind you the car had collapsed around me funnily enough my eyes were wide open, those dark penetrating eyes almost as if I were the one who was assessing what was going on. Apart from cuts to my face from the glass that didn't seem to be marked but the rest of it was just a tangled mess of clothes seeped in blood, glass, fragments of the car, papers I had in the car. All I saw were what looked like a paramedic who crawled under the lorry and dragged my body out as best he could. I felt a bit sorry for him he was only young still I guess it was his job; he must get used to these things.

I remember a young doctor that I worked with at the surgery being very upset when there was a bad accident actually outside the surgery that he had to attend. He was terribly shaken with it.

However, they took my body out, popped it into the ambulance. A doctor came and said I was dead and another policeman went with me to the mortuary. My car was pulled out and left to one side.

They transported the lorry away, presumably to check the tachograph was in order. I assume they have a police vehicle examiner to look at it. I knew instinctively that he hadn't done too many miles and felt sure he was a good driver. The man in question was given a breath test which proved to be negative, his phone was checked and even though he had many calls on it from various women (seemed to be all women ringing him!) There were no text messages apart from incoming so as regards that he was clear. The lorry had been kept in a yard at home he said. They really put him through the mill as I watched from the corner of the ceiling of the interview room of the police station. Once again I wanted to put my arms around him and tell him everything was going to be all right. I knew instinctively that he was innocent and that it was just an accident.

One of the policemen was called away, talking quite softly on the phone, so much so I couldn't hear what was being said. There was something that had happened whilst the policeman was out of the room. I could feel the change in the atmosphere

The tone of the questioning changed also. "Who had access to the vehicle? Where were the keys kept?"

Seemed a bit strange- then came the fact that the examiner had found that the brakes had been tampered with, there was a hole in the brake pipe, very small but it was there. It was put there for a reason; someone knew what he or she was doing. They asked if he had any enemies to which he said he didn't know of any. They wanted to know where he had come from, who he had seen over the past few weeks, which proved to be difficult for him to answer. He had so many women he used to keep in contact with, some with husbands some without. They were all just friends he insisted, of course the policeman didn't believe him you could tell by his face, the more they examined the phone the more obvious it was they were constantly calling and texting him as far as they were concerned he was up to something didn't know what but he was certainly guilty of something. He was too full of himself; he looked as if he could take care of himself as well. There was even a suspicion that he was into something giving him a chance to confess.

He kept insisting that this was not the case saying that he liked women, he met them online, talked to them and eventually he used to see them and they would always end up in bed with him without much persuasion. The police didn't like this attitude at all. The lack of respect from him as regards women, and it was obvious that as he had the lorry he could travel all over the country to meet them under the guise of working, different bed every night was the implication.

Oh dear, he was in trouble, not from the accident but from his life style. So begins the long and arduous task of sifting through all the women. They start off with the ones he is seeing at present. He doesn't like it at all, anger coming to the surface, he really doesn't want to answer their questions. As far as he is concerned it is his business who he sees and what he does but the police suspect him of more than just seeing different women. They certainly think he is covering up something more sinister. The policeman is called away again and when he comes back his face tells a lot. Something else has happened, something much more serious. They question him more about where he is heading but he will not say.

They check his phone; from this they discover each of their addresses and start nearby with Basingstoke where he knows someone called Suzannah He had spent a long time talking to her in the past so they assumed they were still friends. They ring her and the phone just keeps ringing. An officer is sent round to her home to make some enquiries. When he arrives he is shocked to see the police already there ahead of him talking to a young man who turns out to be her son. Suzannah was in an accident on the A30 today and was killed instantly when a lorry lost control and ploughed into her car he was informed.

At this point I realised they were talking about me and that took some time for me to take it on board, they were definitely saying I was dead although how they could think that I don't know. I could hear everything they were saying and even though they couldn't hear what I was saying I was determined that I would find a way to communicate with them. My poor son David was stood there not believing what he was told. He let them in the flat so that they could talk privately as so many of the neighbours had come out wanting to know what had happened. They were a caring lot my neighbours were.

The young policeman took a few minutes for this information to penetrate his brain; the local office that was dealing with the accident in question had sent him. Was the lorry driver coming to see her? The plot thickens! Now, he has to pull himself together and deal with the situation and ask some relevant questions of the son, knowing how difficult this is going to be. For goodness sake, he had just heard that his mother had been killed without having all this to deal with as well.

He began by saying how sorry he was to hear about his mother's death and apologised for bothering him at such a time but explained that he needed to know certain things if he had any information that he could share with them it would be very helpful. The only thing that David knew was that his mother had a relationship with someone called Danny from Dudley last year. It lasted for 11 months and he knew his mother hadn't seen Danny since the previous November. He felt sure she was still speaking to him on the phone but that was all. When asked why it ended he didn't know, something must have really upset her for her to have finished it as she really cared for this man. He wasn't the sort of person she normally went for but there was something between them that was special or at least she thought that. The policeman asked if he could take away the computer from the flat, he knew that the phone was with her in the car, maybe he could get something from that that would help. It was not an ideal situation but he had been as sensitive as possible with David. He had allowed him to take the computer away so that they could get some idea of what had been going on.

I was not amused, that was my computer with all my private things on it! I tried to think what was on it but I am afraid my brain seemed muddled suddenly, probably because I had hit my head on the wheel when the lorry ploughed into me. I was reeling going around in circles, my head was spinning, I suddenly felt very tired and exhausted actually I felt as if I could sleep for a week.

When I came out of the haze I was in it struck me that they must be talking about Danny, as he was the only person from the midlands that I knew. What on earth was he doing on the A30 that morning? Was he coming to see me or someone else? I had reached the stage where I didn't know what to believe. I wasn't expecting him so why would he just turn up? I suppose anything is possible with him, he had lied and cheated his way through our relationship even though I didn't know it at the time so I supposed he could turn up unexpectedly, I wouldn't put anything past him. This would account for the feelings I had when I wanted to comfort him in the lorry and tell him everything was going to be ok. Guess I am a real softie when it comes to him.

CHAPTER

T he police continued with their questions, they found
women in the local area that he knew, people whom he
had met online. One recounted how they had met up in
a pub had a few drinks but she decided he wasn't for her. She was
quite snooty and said that his tattoos had put her off. When the
police called at her house she was in a hurry to get rid of them.
The reason for this soon came to light when her husband came
home. Of course she denied everything including all the phone
calls that they had made to each other, many of them were late at
night when her husband was working away from home. Distance
was the big problem for them he was in the Midlands and she in
the South East.

They travelled south because one of the women lived near Southampton. When they arrived they realised that this one had money, lots of it. It was a beautiful house with landscaped gardens, tall poplar trees surrounding it. She was charming, told them she was very lonely since her children were away at boarding school and her husband who was a banker was abroad working. He went away for three months at a time and she was left alone. Of course she had people who would visit but apart from the housekeeper and her husband who helped in the garden they were the only people that she saw on a regular basis. She was very grateful for the time that Danny spent with her, she knew he was busy but he did manage to come down for a few days every month. She thought he was wonderful, very helpful when she needed someone to talk to anytime day or night. They had long conversations about their respective children, he told her about one of his grandchildren who was being bullied at school and she had arranged for him to be taught at his home by a tutor and the boy was doing very well indeed. He hoped to go on to Naval College in a few years. It was very exciting and good for her to feel that she had helped in some small way. They asked how they had met and she confirmed that it was an online site where she had joined in the hope of finding someone to go out with in the evenings. Unfortunately, he never seemed to want to go out anywhere. She liked the theatre and museums didn't mind going to garden centres when necessary. She also loved playing tennis in the summer but couldn't see him doing that. In fact they had very little in common in fact but she liked him, he made her laugh. She knew that it would have to end once her husband came back, he certainly would not approve of her with him. She loved her husband very dearly and hopefully she would end it before he returned. She hadn't told him about their yacht that was moored near Southampton, felt it best not to. This one had her head screwed on the correct way thought the policeman. In actual fact she was using him in many ways.

They travelled to Oxford to meet some one called Teresa. She was very pretty, very petite, dark haired very young looking. The police were a bit dubious about asking this one questions about Danny. After all he was in his late 60's at the time and it didn't seem right that he was going after very young girls. However, she assured them that she was in her 40's and he used to come down at nighttime, stay for a few hours and then go home. It was a very strange way of behaving and the police couldn't believe that someone could get away with it. This had been going on for a few years apparently. She thought he was faithful to her.

The next place they went was Corby Northants. They arrived at a cottage and were greeted by a very nice lady very neat about 75/80 years old. Of course she knew him, yes he would visit her quite often bringing her flowers and chocolates. No, he was not a relative she had met him in the local post office one day when he stopped for something to eat on the way back to Dudley. She knew all about him, about his unhappy childhood being brought up in a children's home about being fostered and being taken back to the orphanage then being fostered again by the same people. He was quite happy there but then he found out that his birth parents were still alive and together and they had had more children. He used to talk for hours to her she said making it seem as if she was the only one he had spoken to. The police had to ask whether they were having any sort of relationship to which she answered, rather indignantly "Yes of course we were!" This they were quite surprised, as she seemed to be a gentle old lady almost like a great grandmother! "He obviously liked variety," muttered one of the policemen!

Then they went as far as Derbyshire. They called in a pub and a big buxom woman came out "Can I help you" she said. The policeman stood there quite taken aback with the latest. I guess she was in her late 40's but obviously very much in control. She said she knew him, they had had an affair a few years ago before she met her present husband but had decided he was just mucking her around so she had pulled out, and she still spoke to him though. Yes, the police knew this already, they had seen the phone massages from her! They were really quite revealing, telling details of what she would like to do to him and visa versa. They asked if he had any other connections in the area to which she answered there was a man who came to see him in the pub to drop something off, a parcel that as he was in the area he had collected from him. She didn't know any further details.

The hunt continued, they found he had several connections in and around Birmingham but there was one woman who spoke very highly of him saying what a nice person he was! At this point I was screaming at them to take a closer look at her house, I knew something was going on there were several parcels in the spare room. Something made them stop and turn around. They asked if they could look around her house, she refused which was her right they had to get a search warrant if they wanted to look around.

She became rather irate at this point, telling them she had done nothing wrong and why question her about Danny he was a good friend of hers. They told her they had reason to believe he had done something wrong or words to that effect but they left the house. They waited outside to see what happened! They are not silly after all I was thinking to myself. Sure enough a van turned up a man got out and walked to the house. The next minute he came out with boxes under his arm. They weren't very large boxes but the police decided to check what was in them. They found quite a large quantity of drugs. They then got their search warrant and in the house they found so much stolen property as well as more drugs. They were both arrested and charged with possessing drugs with intent to supply it on the open market and also receiving stolen goods. I did wonder whether the parcel that Danny had collected from the man in the pub was one of these boxes??

They continued up to Yorkshire next, there were several women to choose from. One of them was a farmer's wife who was full of the joys of spring. They went with her whilst she got the cows in for milking. She informed them that Danny used to come and see her often. They used to meet up in the barn where the cows were in fact; he had helped her with the milking on a few occasions. She used to sneak out as her husband was usually tired by this time of night. She was quite open about Danny saying they had sex in the barn with all the animals watching them. She pointed out that her husband gave up years ago and couldn't satisfy her anyway. So, she put an advert on one of the dating sites with an old picture of her when she was younger and of course Danny latched on to this.

She reckoned she was insatiable. She was quite a large lady who didn't give a damn what she said to them in fact she kept her eye on one of the policeman. She was attracted to him and made it quite obvious what she wanted. The only thing of interest to the police it seemed was when they asked if he had ever stored anything with her at the farm. She told them that he had stored some boxes at one point but her husband had found them and decided it was probably old farm equipment he had stored for so many years. He took it all to a reclamation yard he knew. He didn't bother opening the boxes at all and she couldn't argue with him. After all it was his shed where they were stored. When Danny came to see her next he was very upset, she saw his temper rising that day and with a bit of hindsight realised what she could have got herself into.

They interviewed more women, most of them were convinced Danny was a lovely man who had fallen in love with them and wanted to spend the rest of his life with them. Without exception this was how they felt.

Needless to say it felt like a kick to my stomach, it was so painful for me and pretty sick also what I was hearing. The fact that me like a stupid child had fallen for him, hook, line and sinker. I believed all the lies he told me but as soon as I had found out he had been lying to me I pulled away and my pride wouldn't let me go back.

# CHAPTER

**T**hey moved up country and eventually found a woman who by all accounts he had been with him for over 5 years. They had done so much together She owned caravans up on the coast where they used to meet as she couldn't go back to her home as her family were not too keen on him, they had told her to get rid and keep away from him. They couldn't see her being happy with him long term which was a joke really if he had been with her for all those years. I did wonder why they had never married but I guess it is for them to know. It has nothing to do with me. She did talk though to the police, explaining that she had spent a lot of money on him over the 5 years, holidays etc that she had paid for. She had bought him some lovely things as well but that was expected if they were together all that time. They fought a lot; very different to my relationship with him I should add. We were just very close and all the time laughing and happy. Things were good between us; we used to fall into each other's arms whenever we saw each other. How things change. I didn't have a lot of money when I first met him, I had just bought the flat and obviously all my money went on that expense but anyway I would not have expected to give him money under any circumstances. I was brought up to believe that was the man's place.

The two detectives were given an address in Glasgow and told to check it out. This was not one of the women this was something different. This was strange address as it was not a house but in middle of a business area. It was a unit that looked very run down. They pressed the bell and a man answered with a quizzical look on his face "Yes what do you want?" he asked. The policeman called Ken said that they needed to talk to him. He was very reluctantly let them in. They entered a very dirty, run down room, they didn't know quite what to expect. Something was definitely going on, their haunches were up. He wouldn't face them at all, kept looking away. Funnily enough towards the door he was obviously expecting someone to turn up.

Someone did, they didn't have to wait too long. He was a strange looking man dishevelled, dirty almost like a tramp. He spoke with an accent, not Scottish almost Slavic sounding. He was not very pleasant at all. He wanted to know whether the other man had his order? "Yes, of course" said the first guy and proceeded to take a box down. With this Ken took over insisting that the box be opened. This is when the second man pulled a knife on him but he wasn't quick enough for the two policemen. They wrestled with him, got him on the floor, put handcuffs on him, then read him his rights and told him he was arrested. At the same time the other chap had moved away from the fracas. Whether he was going to run I didn't know but he didn't get a chance. Ken and his partner decided that they had better look in all the boxes that were stored.

When they opened the first one they found a quantity of cards, credit cards and debit cards, from every bank imaginable, in fact there were so many all with different names on them. It was quite obvious what was going to happen to them. They were going to be cloned in someway or other.

The other boxes that were opened contained cigarettes and tobacco. Some of them contained jewellery; cash, which obviously had been stolen. It was just thrown into the boxes and sealed. Very odd I saw what looked like diamonds something I really loved and I longed to touch them and all the gold as well. The other boxes were bigger and contained video games. Someone must have put them there. The chap that was working there didn't know what to say about the haul. There was quite a lot of it. On the open market it must have run into £1000's of pounds. Someone must be collecting it and bringing it to this storage unit and who would have the ideal set up to do this –Danny-Of course. He could arrive without anyone being any the wiser, drop it off and just go away again no one would suspect him of this. He was just delivering after all, calmly collecting, meeting women en route spending the nights with them then coming up here. No one would be any the wiser.

Of course the man who was looking after the store could not give them any names as he didn't know any he said. This was just a job to him he was paid weekly with cash which suited him fine. It was always there every week he would receive an envelope with the cash in it pushed through the letterbox. He never saw who delivered it. When asked how he got the job he had been told on the phone that if he wanted it he could have it provided he could be there on the Monday morning when the door would be left open, the keys were inside and he was given instructions, again on the phone about deliveries. A very strange set up.

When the police checked into his background they found that he had a series of burglary connections to his name, he had been in trouble since he was a teenager first petty things leading up to quite violent things. There was nothing there that they could charge him with at the moment but they warned him they could be back and this time he could be charged with receiving stolen goods. Slowly the police were building up a case but it really was going very slowly but they really felt they were on to some big ring of people who were instigating all this to happen. It was just a shame that someone had taken it upon them selves to try and cause Danny some problems and possibly kill him whist they were at it. Seemed a bit extreme to me.

They continued with their enquires and went across to Wales where the story was much the same as before. There seemed to be a few people with the name Jane that kept cropping up. Some of the women were quite pleasant to talk to, even though some of them bawked at what they were told which really shouldn't have happened but I am afraid by this time the police dealing with it had heard the story so many times they really didn't care. He was a philanderer there was no doubt of that but no one had the inclination to do him harm, quite the contrary really. They all maintained that he was the love of their lives; they all wanted a future with him.

He had a few more in Wales one of whom had never met him but had continued a relationship with him online, as he couldn't find the time to visit her. She was very gullible I thought but when she was told what he was like she reacted with avengance saying what she would do to him if ever she came in contact with him. Again, there was no reason to suspect she wanted him dead and it was obvious that even though she was angry with him I didn't think she would ever have hurt him. I could see the tears that were welling up and I must say felt so sorry for this one.

There was another one in Cannock that he knew but this one had only just come to light. She had sent a text to him that day saying the time she would be down in Dudley. They trouped down to Dudley to meet her, as they hadn't at this point been to his house. When they reached the house and knocked on the door they were greeted with a woman in her mid to late 70's she looked nothing like most of the other women he went with. She said he wasn't there; it wasn't her house she had only just arrived to visit as she did every week. I must say I was a bit shocked to hear this, the reason I had finished the relationship last year was that I found out he was writing to his ex because she rang me and told me and various other things as well but I never suspected this. How long had this been going on for, Ken asked, "Oh over a year" she said in response. She came down to see him on a regular basis; they were in love they were getting married. I laughed at this I really did. You poor woman I thought. They asked where he was and she replied he had gone to see someone down south an elderly lady who had a lot of problems that he was trying to help her with. She thought her name was Susan or Suzannah. Apparently he used to talk to her quite often but would take the phone upstairs. What the hell was this I thought, for a start I was certainly not elderly, not as old as she was, certainly more glamorous, thinner and definitely with less lines on my face. Everyone thought I was younger than my ex husband and he was 10 years younger than me. I have always taken great care of myself; always try to look smart as well. I was very indignant at the description of me. Then I wondered why, there must be an ulterior motive to this madness. It came out why, she had spent so much money and helped him in so many ways anything he wanted she would provide. More fool her I thought to myself.

She also said he had a lock up near to the house where he kept bits and bobs. They wanted the key to check it out. She found it and it was obvious that she was very familiar with the layout of the house. They asked where it was and when they arrived it was like an Aladdin's cave full of televisions an all sorts of electrical goods. Oh dear he was certainly in trouble this time. There had been a spate of burglaries from a number of electrical shops in Birmingham and it looked as if they had stumbled across the proceeds from them.

The needed to question him urgently, they needed to find out just what he was into. They left the woman there knowing full well that the minute their backs were turned she would call him but of course they had the phone. They also knew that his son had been informed already but as this woman wasn't a relative there was no need to inform her. They had just told her that they needed to talk to him as regards ongoing inquires, no doubt she would find out what had happened once they had left.

The travelled back down to the South stopping off at a café en route for their lunch, they were in no hurry, he could wait a while.

They arrived back with all the information they had but something was missing Ken knew it. There was another piece to this mystery that wasn't obvious. All right they had stolen property, lots of it stored in different places, drugs etc but he felt there was something else that wasn't so obvious. They asked him about it all but of course apart from the bare facts he wouldn't give anything away, he was being very cagey. They questioned him re the women and he reckoned none of them were telling the truth. As regards the woman from Cannock she came down sometimes to clean his house for him! Oh the arrogance of it. He insisted he had a girlfriend who lived in Basingstoke and was on his way to see her. I stifled a laugh at this lie.

# CHAPTER

In a quiet residential street in Wolverhampton there was someone screaming ear-piercing screams that sent a shiver down ones spine. One of the neighbours had knocked on the door to be greeted with a young Chinese woman bleeding profusely, her clothes were covered in blood, and she had been stabbed repeatedly. She fell into the neighbour's arms. She helped her away from the house. There was a shuffling coming from inside the house and the woman was very distressed she kept saying what sounded like Mia. All the neighbour could think of was getting her an ambulance. When they eventually arrived they called the police. The young Chinese girl had lost consciousness and they got her into the ambulance and kept an eye on her as they got her to A & E.

The police meanwhile had stormed into the house knocking the person who answered the door over. As he lay on the floor the police noticed another body half way into another room. They quickly checked who else was in the house but there was no one. They looked upstairs and found a lot of sleeping bags scattered around.

At that point another police car was coming down the road to join them just in time to see at least 20 young girls fleeing via the back door of this house. They gave chase; some of them gave up running voluntarily but some got away.

The other body was a young girl who had obviously been badly beaten. She looked so young and innocent. What on earth had they stumbled upon I wondered.

They continued searching the house, finding that the whole of the roof space was filled with cannabis plants. They had fixed the electric meter so that it came from the main grid; they needed the heat for the cannabis plants of course. As these plants have to have to have moisture as well as light the loft needed to be kept at one temperature all the time. It felt wet and sticky and a horrible smell came from the plants. There were so many of them. It was like a greenhouse in hot summer with no fresh air to breathe.

The man they threw on the floor had got up and tried to make his escape unsuccessfully. They tried to question him but he kept saying he didn't speak English and even though the police did not believe him there was very little they could do about it. They arrested him and took him to the local police station where he could sit in a cell and ponder his decision not to speak English.

As far as the police were concerned this was a vice den, the girls were all young and from China or somewhere quite close. They tried to question the ones they had managed to catch but of course they all said the same thing that they didn't speak English. Eventually they bought in a woman to translate and even though they were very frightened it transpired that they had been brought here to study English so that they could become translators in their own country, which was Thailand. They came over approximately 6 months ago. They all came from a remote area of Thailand and they were all enthusiastic about coming over to our country even though they had travelled over in a very strange way. They had a large van take them to the airport, their fares were paid for them but when they reached this country they were bungled into another van and brought to the house. From then on they were told that they had to work before they could begin to learn English and of course their passports were confiscated. This meant that they had to be ready at all times to do whatever was required of them. The girl who was found dead objected to going with this dirty man and he hit her, then raped her twice then hit her some more. She hit her head on the door as she fell to the ground. The other girl had tried her best to support her when he turned on her. Fortunately she managed to scream loudly enough for someone to hear her and come to the house.

The girls said they were not allowed out of the house at all. Food was brought in for them if they were ill medicine was given to them. Whether it was the correct medicine they didn't know. All that they knew was that they were prisoners in the house with very little chance of getting away. Usually there were a couple of strong men there making sure that they didn't escape. The only work they had to do apart from looking after the men they had to serve was the plants in the loft area – they had to make sure that they were watered and kept at a constant heat. As they had only been confined to the house for so long they didn't know what the future held for them. They really should think themselves lucky that the police had been called as they could have been kept there a long time never seeing the light of day or their families ever again.

I couldn't understand how Danny was involved in this latest thing. I guess it will come out eventually. I did so hope he wasn't involved, as I never thought of him as being violent in any way. Well, he certainly wasn't to me anyway.

Time seemed to march on. The girls in the house were all interviewed over and over again. None of them were eligible to live in this country so were classed as illegal immigrants and eventually they would be deported. They were being treated quite well; at least they were away from the house.

# CHAPTER

anny was interviewed again but denied all knowledge of the girls. Yes he had been to Wolverhampton on several occasions not that he could remember the last time he was there. Must have been six months ago he guessed when he delivered a van to a house. It was done for a friend he explained it was full of frozen food, the doors were locked from the outside to prevent any contamination. He thought it was meat that was being imported and that it had to be kept at a certain temperature. He had picked it up at an address in Dover and dropped it off in Wolverhampton. Couldn't remember the address, though.

The police seemed happy enough with his explanation, I wasn't, but still! I didn't know what he was capable of doing with all the lies he had told me in the past just to cover his tracks. Always a partial lie not a complete one. I was beginning to think there was a lot to Danny that I just had no idea about. He was quite a character and I guess one cannot know a person after 11 months particularly if that person is clever and has repeatedly lied to you. One day he will slip up and say something incriminating that was for sure. I can remember a time when he told me a lie and when I confronted him he changed the story completely not admitting what he had done just changing it to suit himself. He was quite something, still I guess if one lies often enough the person get to believe that is what has happened. By the time this happened I had checked up on Narcissism and what I know of it is that they mirror the person they are with at the beginning. If you are empathetic all the better. They are the devils at home and angels in company and as I lived with my ex husband for over 30 years I do know what I am talking about. Even though at the time I didn't realise what it was all about it is only since that I have taken the trouble to study Narcissism and really begun to understand it. Women have to constantly give them reassurance that they are loved, they do become obsessed with certain people constantly checking where they are and what they are doing. At the same time they will have a few women on the side, as back up should the present one fail them in any way. They are quite capable of removing someone from their home and replacing her the same day. Not a pretty picture at all. Maybe they cannot help it, maybe it is to do with their childhood but it certainly has a far reaching effect on someone who cares for them. They then will flaunt the new person on social media etc to make the original person jealous. If they decide to return to the original woman they will make a big effort to win her back then revert to the original behaviour.

Having said all that I cared a great deal for him. I knew he wasn't good for me and even though I had walked away he still had the ability to draw me back. As I have said before I have not seen him since the previous November and it is now May that makes six months. He is very difficult to get over. I tried blocking him on everything apart from emails. Then he sent abusive emails that were not very nice. He did apologise for this on umpteen occasions and of course I fell for it. I just do not know how someone can be lovely one minute and then change so rapidly if he doesn't get his own way. He certainly is a mystery. Mind you, I must say if he was so involved in all the things the police had found out he must have been absolutely exhausted no time to do anything let alone hold on to a relationship. It certainly looked like that though.

I find it very hard to believe that he could do anything violent but maybe I am kidding myself.

They did more investigations on the lorry and it was proved that someone had messed with it –they had made a small hole in the brake pipe, not clearly visible but it had been proved that it was done by inserting maybe a sharp object into it perhaps the sort of thing that one checks to see if a cake is cooked right through. I know I have used one on several occasions in the past to check my cakes. He was aware that I cooked a lot having made him several things in the past. This was deliberate though someone wanted him dead!

He had quite a large family in the midlands and I don't think they would be very pleased to hear that someone wished their father dead.

Up in Dudley, the woman waited until the police had left and immediately rang his son who informed her he had been in an accident that involved a fatality. She was extremely worried by this, going through her mind at that moment was the fact that if he was in trouble with the police he wouldn't be back in the near future and she wanted him there right now. See, I was able to pick up her thoughts at that moment and they were quite graphic. She obviously enjoyed sex with whoever was handy at the time and had come down to see him for that purpose and the fact that he wasn't there to satisfy her needs was making her angry.

His son Martin thought about the phone call he had just received and it felt very strange to him. Why was this woman down in Dudley when he knew for a fact that his father was in the south and had planned to have a few days away with his girl friend. He had met this woman on a couple of occasions but only in passing and he was sure his father would have filled him in if there had been any sort of relationship. It puzzled him enormously.

Why would she be there to begin with? Why would she have travelled down from Cannock if she knew he wasn't there? He tried to remember if there was anything else he could bring to mind and the only thing was the fact that she had been a lorry driver for many years and obviously knew what went on under the bonnet of a lorry. This worried him a little as the police had told him that the brake pipe had been sabotaged. It would have to have been done by someone who knew what he or she was doing. He rang his sister and spoke to her re his worry. She immediately said that he had to inform the police straight away and if he didn't she would.

He rang the police and they sent someone up to question her more thoroughly. When was she last down there etc? It turned out that she had come down a couple of weeks ago and had asked him if she could drive his lorry to the petrol station to fill it up for him. That seemed innocent enough but what it did prove was that she had access to it alone. After further questioning it turned out she knew a lot about him and his girlfriends, she knew he had people visiting him because he would tell her to go home. She walked them round the property and pointed out all that she had paid for over the past 18 months and it was quite a lot. Apparently she had helped with the digging of the pond, filling it with Koi Carp and plants, laid the slabs even though he had dug the ground below, bought the shed, and so much else. In fact she said that at one point she felt like burning the shed down, as he was so ungrateful.

Slowly they began to realise that she certainly had an ulterior motive. They came to the conclusion that she was capable of doing so many things. She drove a lorry in the past, she had knowledge of the mechanics of it, he had spun her a line which was very cruel and more than anything she was very jealous, insanely so. They questioned her more about the house about when he moved there which wasn't so long ago, less than a year ago as it turned out.

They took her fingerprints and proved that she had touched the brake pipe. With that she flew into a rage, telling them that he had used her and what did he expect? She was determined to destroy him. She had every intention of setting fire to the house and the shed she didn't care anymore. She loved him so much and this was the way he treated her. She had decided that the best thing to do was for him to have an accident and then she would be there for him, to care for him. This way he would rely on her so much that eventually he would marry her. As it was she had caused the accident and unwittingly had caused my death. They charged her with manslaughter.

The police were still not satisfied and Ken well he kept on fishing for something else. There had to be he could feel it in his bones. He decided to check out the house more thoroughly. Upstairs he found a lot of things that belonged to women, a lot of clothes etc. When he looked in a cupboard there was a suitcase and when he opened it he was surprised. There was enough clothing, soap things, make up, a purse that had no money in it but it did have some identification of a woman called Sally Taylor. This was odd Ken felt, why would this woman leave her clothes etc at the house or maybe this was one of his women. On the identification they found what looked like an address in Blackpool. This they checked out only to find that she had gone missing six months previous. This was what Ken was looking for; he knew it at that moment.

Over the next few hours the whole road was out looking at what was going on. It was a quiet neighbourhood everyone knew everyone else or thought they did. They brought in Cadaver dogs and they obviously sensed there was something under the ground. They dug up the garden, or more to the point they moved all the slabs and started digging around the point where the dogs had shown the most interest. Funnily enough this was very near to the shed. If they started digging up around that they would surely have to empty it first as it was packed with things, I knew that from 7 months ago. They dug up a beautiful tree I had given him I shuddered to think what could be under it.

Then they found her or what was left of her.

I found this terribly difficult to understand, how could he? What on earth did she do to warrant this? It must have been something that threatened him for him to take such a step?

They removed the body to undergo forensics examination.

His son turned up at the house, very distraught eager to know what had happened. He knew his father and he knew he hadn't done this dreadful thing. He loved women-yes he did but as regards killing someone he just couldn't believe it. He was questioned quite extensively and the only person that had been to the house was the woman who had already been arrested for my demise. They asked him to think back to Christmas time approximately 6 months previously. He then remembered that his father had taken a trip just before Christmas to Ireland fishing that seemed a bit odd but there are certainly places where one can fish in Ireland all the year round. He thought it was probably Pike he caught; he knew that there was a photo of him somewhere. He also liked sea fishing.

That was it Ken was determined to get to the bottom of this so he returned to base and began questioning the woman who was called Jennifer Brown. At first she denied it but looking at her he knew he was on to a sure thing. She was well built whereas the description of Sally Taylor was that she was tiny, a slip of a girl in her late 20's

She explained to them what happened, as she was not feeling very strong at this point.

Jealousy was the motive she eventually confessed to killing her and burying her in the garden. He apparently had dug the ground over and had put the shed there earlier in the year and had left part of the ground for planting. When he returned he had thanked her for sorting it all out. What she had done was laid more slabs and just left enough room to put the plant in above the girl.

Sally had arrived one Saturday evening and she had been there, she obviously thought that he would be there. Unfortunately she had encountered Jennifer, they sat and talked for a while where Sally explained to her that she was having Danny's baby. Jennifer absorbed this fact very slowly and then she spelt it out for her that she, Jennifer, was about to marry Danny. With this Sally laughed she couldn't believe it. This was too much for Jennifer she lashed out at her sending her reeling across the room. She hit her head on the coffee table that was glass and wood and fell to the floor. It certainly didn't take much to kill her; the blow must have been delivered with quite a lot of force. Jennifer did check that she wasn't breathing. She then dragged her into the shed overnight. She had to do something with the body, she knew that much. Obviously she couldn't start digging late at night so she decided to wait until the morning before digging in the garden. In the meantime she locked the house took the keys with her and took Sally's car. She knew there was a place where she could dump it in water in a lake that he had shown her months before. She wasn't thinking straight at all the only thing that she needed to do was get rid of the car and the body but very stupidly she didn't think of putting Sally in the car as well.

She returned an hour later; everything was just how she had left it. She made herself a cup of tea and sat down and thought. Her brain was so mixed up at that point; she knew she couldn't have possibly allowed this woman to have his baby, no way. He was going to marry her that was all there was to it. She slept for a while, a restless sleep which was hardly surprising. She never thought for one moment that she was doing anything wrong, she was just stopping Sally in her tracks. Then she saw Sally's bag and case in the corner. She decided she would sort that out later, tomorrow maybe. She then looked on Sally's phone and there were so many messages from Danny to her telling her how much he loved her and couldn't wait to be married to her. With this knowledge Jennifer cried, she sobbed her heart out, this was unbelievable. She knew he had been with someone for many years prior to her meeting him but she never guessed that he had obviously having an affair with this Sally girl all along. This made her very angry; he was obviously two timing her. Well, no more, she had to get her revenge somehow. On one hand she wanted to hurt him badly on the other hand she loved him so much and as far as Sally was concerned she had laughed at the thought of the two of them together, she had actually laughed which was terribly hurtful.

The only thing left to sort out was the case; she decided to put it up in the airing cupboard for the time being. Martin suddenly appeared as she was packing the case away. He asked why she was there? She told him she had arranged with Danny to come down and clean the house. He said he had come to pick up something from upstairs in the house. Thank God, she thought to herself he doesn't need to go in the shed.

In the early hours of the morning she went out and carefully dug a hole in the ground. It was very quiet outside but with the moonlight she managed to do it. She put Sally into the hole and threw some soil over her. She decided she would finish it off the following day when she could see more clearly. There was always a chance that Martin would come back and need to go into the shed and she couldn't risk that happening. She fell into Danny's bed that night going straight to sleep exhausted.

The following day dawned and she knew that she had to complete what she had started to do the night before. The ground that morning was hard as a frost had set in overnight. It became quite difficult to lay the couple of slabs needed. She saw the plant and decided to move that over so that the roots would take a hold.

Danny came back later that day he asked whether there had been any phone calls or had anyone been to the house and she answered no, no one. He then took himself upstairs and and rang Sally but of course Jennifer had the phone in her pocket, she had thought to switch it off the night before. He then sent a text wanting to know where she was. No reply needless to say.

Life carried on for several months, Danny came to the conclusion that Sally had walked out on him, and maybe she had somehow got wind of the other women and decided to go. He didn't know and of course she had been very cagey about giving him her home address in Blackpool. Her parents were elderly and didn't know about him. He had never met anyone from her family so had no one to ring apart from her phone which 6 months down the line she still wasn't answering so he decided that she wasn't worth bothering about.

Jennifer was still coming down to see him, he was still sleeping with her, he had reached the stage where he felt he was doing her a favour once every few weeks but he got no pleasure from it at all.

The alarm clock rang rather loudly in my ear. I woke up with a terrible headache, probably one of my migraines and went to get out of bed. In that moment my dream came back to me, my goodness what on earth was I thinking, it just showed what an effect that Danny had on me. It was so vivid I could remember everything so clearly. The doorbell went and I staggered to answer it. There stood Danny with a bunch of flowers in his hand he flung his arms around me gave me a big kiss and said he decided at 5 o'clock this morning that he would come and see me. I was not at my best that morning. I felt shattered; the dream was so real I could have been there. I have never been very good first thing in the morning but this morning I was terrible. I told him to make himself a cup of tea or coffee whilst I had a shower and washed my hair. I felt terrible. However, I got myself showered and dressed and tried to explain what had happened in my dream. He of course, thought it was stupid what I had been dreaming of. It was so real though.

He then announced that we were going away for a few days, wouldn't tell me where to but suggested that I pack some trainers for walking and some loose clothes. We got into the car and he set off down the M3 towards Southampton. It became quite clear to me where he was heading, the island of course.

As we reached the ferry Danny said to me right we are going to do everything that you want from now on to which I laughed at him-that would be the day it certainly would.

Having been brought up in Derbyshire one of my wishes was to live overlooking the sea. Yes, Derbyshire was beautiful, the wildness of the moors, the hills and valleys there was so much to see, the one place you could see all the changes of the seasons. I remember many years ago travelling up on a train through the valleys in the autumn, how colourful were the trees all the golds and yellows of the leaves. They made a magnificent sight after I had spent so much time in London. It was just so different.

However, my wish was to be able to buy a cottage on a deserted beach somewhere. I didn't know where or how I was going to achieve it.

At one point I had travelled down to Cornwall, spent Christmas with my son's wife's family. They lived within walking distance to the sea. Of course it could be quite wild down in that part of Cornwall. This has spurred me on to achieving my goals

I had travelled all along the coasts of England, Wales, Ireland, not quite all around Scotland, the Mediterranean, Scandinavia, The

Caribbean and really couldn't decide where I wanted to settle –all I knew was that it had to be by the sea.

I needed somewhere that would see the sunset in the evening, this way I could continue with my photography as well as writing

I loved the Isle of Wight having lived there for two years some time ago. It was charming although at the time because of circumstances beyond my control I couldn't stay. All the people I got to know were very genuine and kind unlike what I had been told. Everyone told me that they didn't like strangers but I never felt that at all. I know they helped me in times of trouble looking after me I couldn't have asked for any more and I was very sad to leave.

I went over there one day in April, not a good day at all. The weather was so miserable. I am afraid I just wanted to walk along the beach where I used to walk with my little dog Che. We used to go along that beach and it was there that I actually got him to go into the water, as he was quite frightened of it. I suspect to a little dog it must have been quite frightening hearing waves making a noise coming towards him. He was a brave little soul though and he did go in after a while. He loved the beach foraging around in the sand. I honestly do not know what he was looking for, I don't think he ever found it but still.

That day the sun was shining, it was June now and we walked along the beach at Sandown toward Yaverland and back again and I felt as if I was coming home again. With or without Danny I had found out where I wanted to be.

Lightning Source UK Ltd.
Milton Keynes UK
UKHW010619171219
355526UK00001B/52/P